John Burningham

MOUSE HOUSE

JONATHAN CAPE • LONDON

For Lily

Some other picture books by John Burningham

Picnic	*Mr Gumpy's Motor Car*	*Husherbye*
Borka	*Mr Gumpy's Outing*	*Granpa*
Tug of War	*Avocado Baby*	*Courtney*
Simp	*The Magic Bed*	*Humbert*
Aldo	*Whadayamean*	*Cloudland*
Where's Julius	*Oi! Get Off Our Train*	*The Shopping Basket*
Come Away From the Water, Shirley	*Edwardo, the Horriblest Boy in the Whole Wide World*	*Time to Get Out of the Bath, Shirley*
Would You Rather?	*John Patrick Norman McHennessy*	*Motor Miles*

JONATHAN CAPE

UK | USA | Canada | Ireland | Australia
India | New Zealand | South Africa

Jonathan Cape is part of the Penguin Random House group of companies
whose addresses can be found at global.penguinrandomhouse.com.

www.penguin.co.uk   www.puffin.co.uk   www.ladybird.co.uk

Penguin
Random House
UK

First published 2017
001

Printed in China
A CIP catalogue record for this book is available from the British Library

ISBN: 978-0-857-55177-1

All correspondence to:
Jonathan Cape, Penguin Random House Children's,
80 Strand, London WC2R 0RL

This is the house . . .

. . . where the family live.
Every evening they have their supper
and then the children go to bed.

But there is another family living in the
house who have to wait until the children
and grown-ups have gone to bed.
Do you know who they are?

They are the mouse family.

The mice have to wait until the humans
have gone to bed before they look for food.

Then the mice can have their supper
and the mouse children can start to play.

The mouse children were told they must
never be seen by the human family.

One evening the boy was on
his way to bed when he said,
"Look, there is a mouse."

The father phoned the mouse catcher.
"The mouse catcher will be here in the morning.
He will get rid of the mice."

"Why do you have to get rid of the mice?"
said the children.
"They don't do any harm."

"They would be all over the house if you let them," said the father. "We must get rid of them." Before they went to bed, the children wrote a message for the mice.

To the mouse family

your lives are in danger

you must get out of the house tonight

from the children

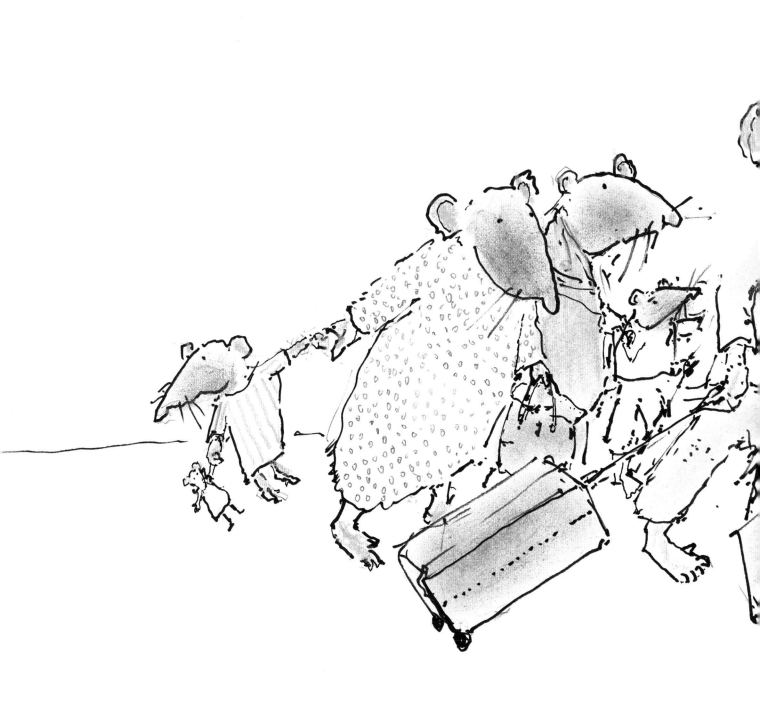

I hear you have a problem
with mice.

I've come to deal
with them.

They get
everywhere.

You won't have any
more mice once they have
eaten my little packets.

In a few days you will be mouse-free.

From their bedroom window, the children could see the mice playing in the garden at night.

They decided to make things
for the mice to play on.

They made a trampoline.

A slide and a swing.

And they would watch the mouse children
playing at the end of the garden.

Now autumn was here,
the leaves were falling and
soon it would be winter.

The snow was on its way.

The children went into the garden
and all the games had gone.
No swings. No slide. No trampoline.
"They didn't even leave a note for us,"
said the little girl.

But, in time, the children soon forgot
about the mice and played their own games.

One night the boy was on his way to bed
when he saw a mouse.

But he said nothing.